Disney · PIXAR

TOY STORY 4

Adapted by Erin Rose Wage

Illustrated by Art Mawhinney

we make books come alive®

pi kids Phoenix International Publications, Inc.

Chicago • London • New York • Hamburg • Mexico City • Sydney

Bonnie's closet doors burst open. The toy town is ready for business! From being the mayor, to running the hat shop, to de-ghosting the haunted bakery, every toy has an important job to do... except Woody. Bonnie doesn't play with him much anymore. He's been left in the closet along with her toddler toys.

While Bonnie's imagination runs free, find these hard-working, and hardly working, toys:

Buttercup   Rex   Dolly   Jessie   Hamm   Woody   Trixie   Buzz Lightyear

At kindergarten orientation, Bonnie is nervous. Woody knows Bonnie is worried about starting school, so he stows away in her backpack in case he can help her. During craft time, Woody sees an opportunity when Bonnie is left without art materials.

Help Woody round up these crafty supplies that Bonnie will use to *make* a new friend...named Forky!

spork

red pipe cleaner

rainbow decal

googly eyes

wooden craft stick

modeling clay

glue

crayons

Forky is Bonnie's favorite toy! He feels most comfortable in the trash, so he hops into every garbage can he finds...and Woody saves him. On a family vacation, the two toys get separated from Bonnie's RV and end up at an antique shop. Woody spots the lamp of his old friend Bo Peep, and he goes searching for her. Instead, he finds Gabby Gabby. Her voice box is broken, and she wants Woody's!

24 HOURS

As Woody stares down Gabby Gabby's ventriloquist dummies, shop around for these antiques:

fondue pot

Gabby Gabby

Benson

birdcage

bonnet

teapot

watering can

trumpet

Woody escapes the antique shop, but Gabby Gabby fork-naps Forky! On a playground outside the shop, Woody encounters a rowdy bunch of Grand Basin Summer Camp kids. Just as he fears for his stitches, he runs into Bo! She's been living as a lost toy with her best pal Officer Giggle McDimples. They agree to help Woody rescue Forky from Gabby Gabby's clutches.

Join in the fun running, stomping, and swinging with these lost, lovable toys:

ice-cream toy

Volcano Attack Combat Carl Jr.

Giggle McDimples

Billy, Goat, and Gruff

Combat Carl Jr.

dinosaur toy

Ice Attack Combat Carl Jr.

Bo Peep

When Woody and Forky have been gone a long time, the rest of the toys in the RV start to worry. Buzz listens to his inner voice and goes in search of his friends. He crash-lands in a carnival, where a carnival worker mistakes him for a prize. Zip-tied to a wall, Buzz meets some colorful characters named Ducky and Bunny, who don't want Buzz taking their top-toy spot.

Before a kid with stellar aim wins them all, look for these premium prizes:

Ducky and Bunny   ice-cream cone   fox   rocket   astronaut   Buzz   yellow star   guitar

Once Buzz finds Woody, the rescue team enters the antique shop together. Down one of the aisles is a pinball machine, which the friends can enter by punching a secret code on the coin return. Inside, tons of toys are unwinding, including Canada's greatest motorcycle daredevil, Duke Caboom! Bo needs him to jump into Gabby Gabby's case, but Duke is nervous. What if he crashes?

Now that Bo has assured Duke that crashing is fine, search through the buzzers and bells for these carefree playthings:

Duke Caboom

Tinny

toy robot

bear with banjo

luchador

collapsible cactus

sea creature

eagle bottle

The rescue turns into a *catastrophe!* When Duke makes the jump, he accidentally crashes and wakes Dragon from a catnap. The commotion alerts Gabby Gabby and her dummies, and soon the toys are scattered...and battered...but they are not giving up!

As Duke finds the courage to distract Dragon, lend a hand to these members of the rescue team:

Forky

Woody

Buzz

Bo Peep

Billy, Goat, and Gruff

Giggle McDimples

Ducky and Bunny

Duke Caboom

Woody gives his voice box to Gabby Gabby in exchange for Forky. He and Forky are happy to have helped her finally find a kid! Their adventure taught them a lot about what it means to be a toy. And as they reunite with the rest of the toys, Forky is perhaps the most excited of all to return to life with Bonnie.

While the friends hug it out, say hello to these oblivious humans:

carnival patron   carnival worker   Bonnie's mom   police officer   Bonnie's dad   Bonnie   security guard   Millie

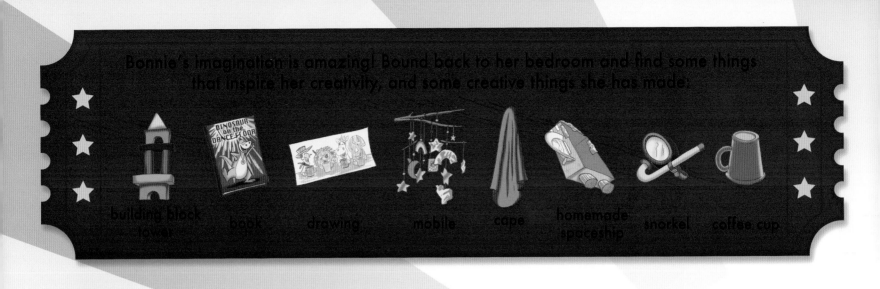

Bonnie's imagination is amazing! Bound back to her bedroom and find some things that inspire her creativity, and some creative things she has made:

building block tower   book   drawing   mobile   cape   homemade spaceship   snorkel   coffee cup

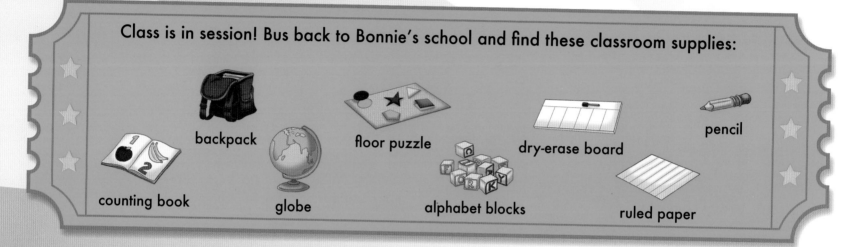

Class is in session! Bus back to Bonnie's school and find these classroom supplies:

backpack   floor puzzle   dry-erase board   pencil

counting book   globe   alphabet blocks   ruled paper

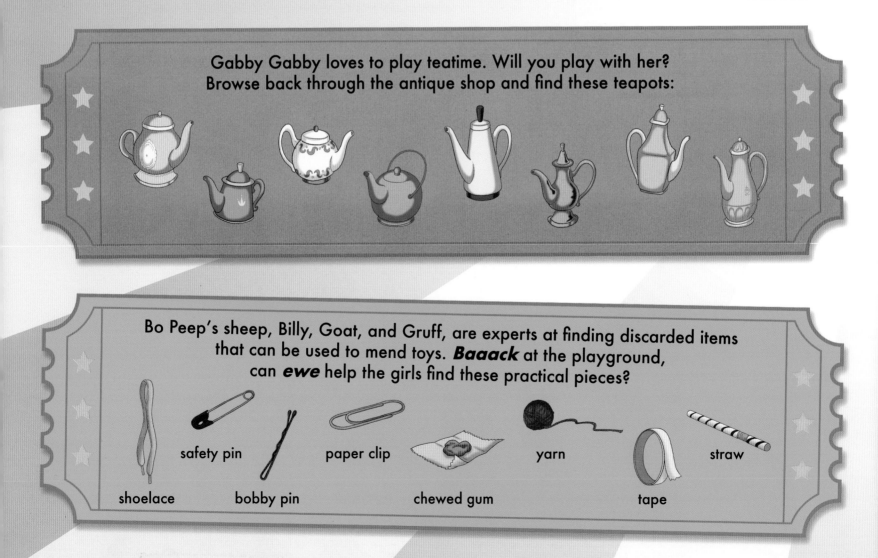

Gabby Gabby loves to play teatime. Will you play with her?
Browse back through the antique shop and find these teapots:

Bo Peep's sheep, Billy, Goat, and Gruff, are experts at finding discarded items that can be used to mend toys. *Baaack* at the playground, can *ewe* help the girls find these practical pieces?

safety pin   paper clip   yarn   straw

shoelace   bobby pin   chewed gum   tape

Practice your aim back at the Grand Basin carnival! To get the bull's-eye, spot each of these things:

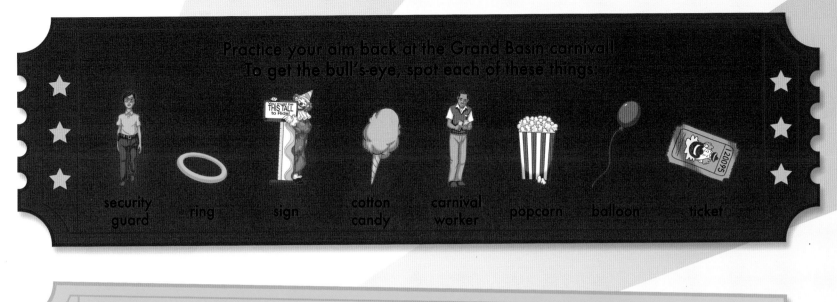

security guard • ring • sign • cotton candy • carnival worker • popcorn • balloon • ticket

Ding! Ding! Ding! Bonus ball! Bump back to the pinball machine and find these doodads:

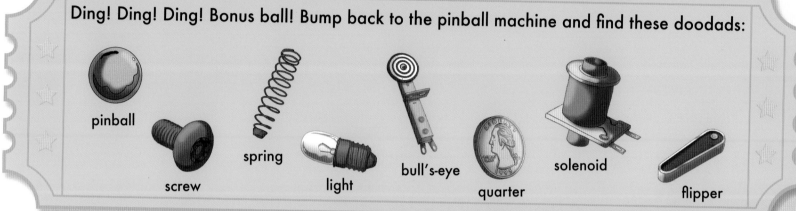

pinball • screw • spring • light • bull's-eye • quarter • solenoid • flipper

Dragon is one feisty feline! Return to the rescue and find these things the cat has clawed or nibbled:

stuffed canary in a birdcage • wooden milk crate • chair • mouse plush • violin • shoe • book • pillow

Step right up to the carnival reunion and find **15** burnt-out bulbs.

Batteries ARE included! Make your way back through the book and find a battery in each scene.

BATTERY